Hank and Fergus

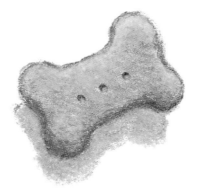

To my beloved son, Oskar — whose vivid imagination
helped mine take flight.
S N-F

For Mika, my dog.
L-A L

Text copyright © 2003 Susin Nielsen-Fernlund
Illustrations copyright © 2003 Louise-Andrée Laliberté

National Library of Canada Cataloguing in Publication Data
Nielsen, Susin, 1964-

Hank and Fergus / Susin Nielsen-Fernlund ; Louise-Andrée Laliberté, illustrator.

ISBN 1-55143-245-5

1. Dogs--Juvenile fiction. I. Laliberté, Louise-Andrée. II. Title.

PS8577.I37H36 2003   jC813'.54   C2003-910449-4

PZ7.N5683Ha 2003

First published in the United States, 2003

Library of Congress Control Number: 2003091862

Summary: When the new boy next door doesn't believe in Hank's invisible dog, Fergus, friendship between the two boys seems impossible. But is it?

Teachers' guide available from Orca Book Publishers.

Orca Book Publishers gratefully acknowledges the support of its publishing programs provided by the following agencies: the Department of Canadian Heritage, the Canada Council for the Arts, and the British Columbia Arts Council.

Design by Christine Toller
Printed and bound in Hong Kong

Orca Book Publishers
1030 North Park Street
Victoria, BC Canada
V8T 1C6

Orca Book Publishers
PO Box 468
Custer, WA   USA
98240-0468

05 04 03 • 5 4 3 2 1

Hank and Fergus

written by Susin Nielsen-Fernlund
illustrated by Louise-Andrée Laliberté

Here's to friends everywhere - real + imaginary!

Susin Nielsen - Fernlund

ORCA BOOK PUBLISHERS

Hank had a dog. His name was Fergus.

Nobody else could see Fergus, only Hank. Some days Fergus was large and hairy; other days he was small and purple with very bad breath.

He was Hank's best friend in the whole wide world.

Fergus hated lima beans, wool sweaters, bath time, bullies and the dark. He loved pillow forts, dinosaurs, bulldozers, mud puddles and bedtime stories.

Hank and Fergus were two peas in a pod.
His parents said, "Don't you think
it's time to make some *real* friends?"

But to Hank, Fergus was
as real as the sun's rays
warming his toes, as real
as the wind rippling
through his hair, as real as
the smell of snow in the
air.

When grown-ups stared, he didn't care because he had Fergus. When big kids called him names, it didn't hurt so much because he had Fergus.

   With Fergus, Hank didn't need any other friends.

Then one day, a new boy moved
in next door.

"Hi, I'm Cooper," said the
boy. "I have a scar on my
stomach 'cause they had to take
my appendix out. Want to see?"

"You stepped on Fergus's tail," said Hank.

"Who's Fergus?" asked Cooper. "And what happened to your face?"

"Come on, Fergus," Hank said. "We're late for lunch."

The next day, Cooper showed up at the park.

    "Seat's taken," said Hank.

    "By who?" asked Cooper.

    "By my dog."

    "What dog? And what's that thing on your face?"

    "Shut up, stupidhead," said Hank.

"You're the stupidhead," Cooper said. "You think that string is
a dog."

 "No, I don't. The string is his *leash*."

 "There's no dog!"

 "Just because you can't see him doesn't mean he isn't
real," Hank replied. Under his breath he added, "Stupidhead."

The next day, Cooper put a sign on his lawn.

The day after that, Hank put a sign on his lawn.

NO COOPERS
ALLOWD

Then he marched Fergus right up to Cooper's sign and started to laugh.

"What's so funny?" asked Cooper.

"Fergus just peed on your sign," giggled Hank.

"Clean it up!" Cooper shouted. Then he stopped himself.

"There is no pee. There is no dog. Just a dirty old piece of string!"
"Let go!" Hank yelled.

Hank and Cooper didn't speak to each other after that.

Hank still had Fergus.

But for the first time, Fergus didn't feel like enough.

Then one day, Hank peeked through the hole in the fence.

"I have something for you," Hank said.

"I have something for you, too," said Cooper.

"It can't ever break," Cooper explained. "Fergus will be safe."
Hank had a lump in his throat. He handed Cooper his gift.

"I thought you might like a dog of your own," he said.

Cooper had a lump in his throat, too. "I've always wanted a pet."

"I was born with this," Hank said, pointing at his face. "It's called a birthmark."

Cooper said, "It looks like a T-Rex."

Hank smiled. "Really?"

"The scar on my belly just looks like a squiggle."

"That doesn't look like a squiggle," Hank said. "It looks like a cobra."

Cooper grinned. "Come on," he said, "let's take these two mutts for a walk."

And as the two boys strolled down the street with their dogs, Hank thought to himself that it might just be possible to have *two* best friends.